For Nilesh, one of my forever friends.
I am blessed with your friendship.
—A.C.

Henry Holt and Company, *Publishers since 1866*
175 Fifth Avenue, New York, New York 10010
mackids.com

Henry Holt® is a registered trademark of Macmillan Publishing Group, LLC.
Copyright © 2017 by Arree Chung
All rights reserved.

Library of Congress Cataloging-in-Publication Data is available.
ISBN 978-1-62779-553-1

Our books may be purchased in bulk for promotional, educational, or business use.
Please contact your local bookseller or the Macmillan Corporate and Premium Sales Department
at (800) 221-7945 ext. 5442 or by e-mail at MacmillanSpecialMarkets@macmillan.com.

First edition—2017 / Designed by Arree Chung and Anna Booth
The artist used acrylic paint on Rives BFK paper, found paper,
and Adobe Photoshop to make the illustrations for this book.

Printed in China by RR Donnelley Asia Printing Solutions Ltd.,
Dongguan City, Guangdong Province
1 3 5 7 9 10 8 6 4 2

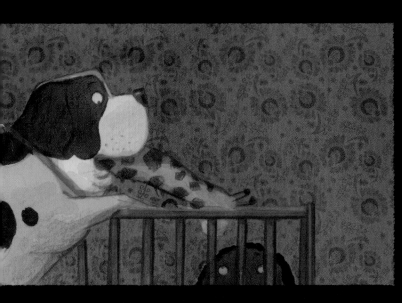